About the Author

Dreena Collins lives in the Channel Isles. Her previous collections include *Bird Wing*, placed as a finalist in the International SPR Book Awards (2020), and *She Had Met Liars Before*, Highly Commended in the Royal Dragonfly Awards, 2021. She has also been published online and within collections, including the Bath Flash Fiction Award and Reflex Press anthologies. She has been listed and placed in several writing competitions.

Dreena published her first novel in 2021, under the pen name 'Jane Harvey.' *The Landlord of Hummingbird House* is modern women's fiction, and won the published novel category of the Eyelands International Awards for 2021.

She is a social media geek (though she hasn't mastered Tik Tok yet). Find more of her work (and wordy memes and quotes) at any of the following:

http://dreenawriting.co.uk/
http://facebook.com/dreenawriting
http://www.instagram.com/dreenawriting
http://twitter.com/dreenac

Embers

(And Other Stories)

Dreena Collins

Twisted Tales of Courage and Comeuppance.

"Courage is resistance to fear, mastery of fear - not absence of fear."

Mark Twain

"Violence does, in truth, recoil upon the violent, and the schemer falls into the pit which he digs for another."

Arthur Conan Doyle

"If you're really a mean person you're going to come back as a fly and eat poop."

Kurt Cobain

Contents

One

Embers

Shortlisted in the Retreat West
Quarterly Flash Competition, 2021.

We are three shades of red. Auburn, copper, sand. Dutifully, we tilt our heads together for the photograph – my sisters leaning in, their long hair falling around my shoulders until we become one tangled mass. Mum is delighted at the sight of their thick manes, disguising my short crop. Susie rests a strand of hair over my head, her cheek pressing hard against mine.

Her hair is closest in colour to dad's. She is a reprint of him, but softer. An echo. It's their turn now, and she laughs when dad suggests she sit on his knee. Eventually, they stand back-to-back, arms folded, propping one another up. Their hair is burnished, metallic. Elizabethan fire.

1

He kisses her forehead after mum takes the picture and then runs back to the barbeque, turning the last few pieces of meat over the dying heat.

Then Susie and Jennifer are together. Jennifer suggests they sit on the rug. Somehow, they know how to pose, how to languish and lounge and laugh in a freeze-frame. There are only eighteen months between them. I am the youngest. The accident.

They ask me to take a picture so that mum can join them. She says no, she couldn't possibly, but it is a half-hearted protest; she is holding her phone out towards me as she says it. I struggle to reach it but say nothing. They sit together, her central, black hair now streaked with grey, skin darker than theirs, jaw stronger - but their three mouths the same. Three perfect smiles grin in unison as I fumble with the button.

Jennifer, still smiling, gets up, takes the phone, and asks me to join them. She comes behind my chair and pushes me over the unforgiving grass. She doesn't wait for my answer: leaves me, planted, behind their stage. She stretches her slender arm up, and out, asks me to duck my head down. But she struggles, and the picture captures only the top of their faces and the bottom of my chin. Briefly, there is a discussion about getting me out of the wheelchair, but this is quickly dismissed as impractical.

Dad says the last of the food is ready, calls us his 'little piggies', snorting. Susie leaps forward and squeezes his torso, tells him he's the porky one. There is a little tussle and tickle, a few nips, and pinches amidst laughter. Dad uses his tongs like lobster claws. She flips up his t-shirt, then breaks away – and they are off. Running, racing across the grass. Mum gasps, giggles, grabs a bottle of water, squeezes it at him as he zips past. Then she and Jennifer are running, too. They are running. Leaping. Laughing.

The discarded meat is turning to charcoal on the rusted embers.

I push my wheels in the mud, calling out, but my words are lost on the wind, my tyres wedged in the ground.

So I watch them, in the distance, as they soar like red kites across the grass.

Two

The Pen

Each time he hurled his insults, Kelly got a new tattoo.

A butterfly when he called her a bitch. A poppy for a pig.

She always had them on her belly: a silent, delicious secret.

Initially, she would go once every month, or two. A slag. A slut. A small black swan. She always saw the same man; looked forward to her visits. Trusted him, in spite of his frown.

"Paint me beautiful," she said. And he understood.

Her tattooist listened as she spoke. He would sketch glass-winged butterflies; stratocumulus clouds. He inked her frame, tangling hydrangeas and vines, wordlessly. They curled around the lumps of her, unfurled across her skin. And she felt a bit bolder each time she left. She felt more like herself.

But as time went on, she had to pick her battles – raise her game. There were too many skirmishes, too little space. Only four-letter words would leave their mark, now, and nothing said with a laugh or a smile.

Of course, him at home, he never knew. At night, if ever he wanted his way, she kept her vest on, and he didn't complain. His rutting was always hurried; eyes squeezed tight in a wince.

Ironic to comment on her body so much, when he never took the time to look, she told her artist, friend, as he chiselled away.

So, he didn't see that she was morphing, winged: etched in dragons and birds. He didn't see that she smiled sometimes. That she no longer recoiled at his words. Her belly still pillowed over the top of her jeans, but she was glad of it these days, pummelled and stroked by her tattooing man.

Eventually, she had to admit that there was no room left. It was over. This would be the last tattoo.

"You choose," she told her sculptor. "You choose me something small but strong."

"I'll paint you, beautiful," he said.

And he did: a tiny wave of letters curling and undulating through the gaps and furrows. Delicate black dots like an army of ants.

Kelly, he wrote, again and again.

Kelly. Kelly. Kelly.

Three
Not So Useless After All

Richard,

Do you remember when I said I was going to take up gardening and you said I was too bloody thick and then you did your yellow phlegmy laugh but this time I ignored you so that made you mad and your face went crinkled yet somehow bloated but you wouldn't admit how furious you were (as that would mean I'd won) so then you were livid because actually the plants grew well so naturally you said my flowers were pointless with a glob of mucus and a twitch and I couldn't understand because they looked like spots of joy and astounded me each morning when their leaves shivered with the weight of dew and promises of the sun yet even though I disagreed I wanted to avoid a row so started planting vegetables too but you hated the vegetables I liked and pretended to gag and puke like a Pantomime Dame while laughing at my purple carrots and refusing them even when they were in a cake a cake a bloody cake and you love cake but you wouldn't even try it so eventually I planted things you liked because I sort of buckled under with your bulk and you ate them just because I didn't say they were mine (ha ha) and I watched and although I am useless and not full of promises and joy like dew and sunshine I had an idea which meant that the next time I cooked I added the worthless flowers Lily-of-the-Valley and Foxgloves and other things you shouldn't eat but honestly you had no idea and then afterwards I buried the remains with the stems and phlegm and puke and then I sprinkled seeds like the babies you never wanted and no one would ever know how bloody clever I was even you you you but I smile anyway while I eat my cake and I watch them sprout because I think I've proved that flowers aren't so useless after all.

Haven't I, Richard?

xxx

Four
The Bride

Here comes the bride.

Dutifully, they stood, craned back to see her entrance. She ignored the congregation, eyes fixed upon the groom. A crowd of bridesmaids tottered around her feet in pinks, yellows, peach. They were a falling mound of macarons.

Debbie twisted her own ring, allowed the light to catch the stone, allowed Ben to hold her other hand. He gripped too tightly, thumb rhythmically brushing back and forth against her hand. His skin was dry. His palm was hot.

Doesn't she look lovely?

They all agreed. Her hair was pinned and scaffolded; dress long and tight. Debbie couldn't imagine ever looking that way: felt claustrophobic, constricted simply by watching her. Her breath caught tight in her gullet, it felt trapped and rough, like a baby's cough. She cleared her throat, swallowed hard, but it remained.

And they couldn't resist – the others - everyone nudging Ben, with a wink and a smile, commenting how he'd be next.

I think I'd like to wait a while.

She whispered it to Tracy, the first time she'd shared the thought out loud. Tracy opened her eyes wide, too wide, but then nodded and said she could do what she wanted, of course. There was no rush. She must do whatever would make her feel happy.

They went through to the reception and the atmosphere shifted: bubbles and snacks and music taking the place of granite and vows. The volume rose around them in a swell and there was laughter, joy. But Debbie felt tense, Ben holding her hand as if she were tethered to him. As if she might run away. Run away. She hated it but needed it, legs jittering and restless in her too-tight shoes.

Debbie said she isn't sure when she's going to marry Ben, you know.

Tracy whispered it to Sandra, who whispered it to Steve. A little ripple in the room, a frisson amongst the chatter.

They sat; they ate. Ben made small talk with someone's childhood friend; Debbie grinned and nodded at a Godparent and two cousins. And by the time they raised a glass to toast the bridesmaids, her words had been moulded, chiselled, painted red across the room.

Debbie said she isn't sure she wants to marry Ben, you know.

Nine o'clock, and people slowly peeled away from the tables to the dance floor. She wondered when she was allowed to leave. She wondered if she had to stay to wave the happy couple off, into the night. A bowling ball in her belly. A baby cough in her throat. Trembling legs. She sat, still. Alone.

Ben was off by the bar, talking, guffawing, when the tittle-tattle came his way.

And she saw him, how he shut down from open to closed – folded in. He looked back to her, aghast, and then he leaned in as they repeated the words, twisted the words, and she knew what they said. She guessed what they said. A choking vine from them to him.

Until he was back. Pale. Still.

Do you want to split up? he asked.

I do, I do, was all she said in reply.

Six
Personal Effects

Up in the attic, amid spiders and dreams, I am unsure where to start. Sorting through everything seems an insurmountable task.

I totter on the beams, toddler-legged and careful, as dad had always instructed. The floorboards weren't strong enough, he said. And I do as I'm told. Always.

No use putting this off any longer.

The place is orderly but caked in snowdrifts of filth. I turn to the suitcases on my left; pull the brown leather one towards me, disturbing a dusty moth.

"Sorry."

Mum always taught me to apologise, and now I say sorry like a reflex. Like a tic. To people; to animals; to inanimate objects. Dead insects. Fifty, one hundred times a day.

Sorry. Sorry. Sorry.

The clasps resist opening, rusted, stiff. Inside, I'm met with photo albums and loose pictures - cascading across one another, jumbled, faded. I move the albums aside, then bundle the loose images up. Mum's face is duplicated in various shades, over again - dad behind the lens. Her, the same, yet different. Ageing, bloating, shrinking over time. She is unsmiling. I allow the photos to tumble, one then another, swiftly, flowing, a waterfall of criticism and memories. I see her, staring, chastising, again and again.

Then I take a bin bag and shovel them in.

Ten minutes later, nothing but a neat stack of albums remains. Jack can have those.

I am lighter. I feel different.

I move on to the next case. I can feel the tips of my fingers slippery and thick with dirt. Its clasps are fiercely sprung, and fire open with a crack. A silverfish flits into the creases of the fabric inside. I do not apologise.

Ha. That's odd.

There is a Christening Gown: browning, crisp. It's the gown Jack wears in the picture on the sideboard. The same one worn by our father before him. I wonder, vaguely, what I wore to my Baptism - where those images are.

Jack would probably want this, I suspect. He has strong feelings on what to keep and what to throw - though not so strong that they extend to helping me. It's not gracious to think this – I know it – but for once, I don't care. He isn't here, after all.

I hold it up – a tangle of impractical ribbons and lace. There is a small stain across the crumpled silk. I probably did that. I rub at it, scratching with my finger on the artificial nap. The weave starts to drift apart. I rub harder until it splits.

"I do apologise," I hear myself say, heavy with sarcasm.

Huh.

It is ugly, it strikes me. And damaged.

I throw it away.

The next suitcase has a zip. It opens with a buzz, smoothly. I am speeding up. In my stride. There are dresses inside – my dresses. Pink. Puffed. Neatly folded and pristine. Fifteen, twenty years old. I suppose I should consider whether Jack wants them for his girls. But no. It does not matter what Jack wants. It doesn't matter.

Hmm. Wait. Does it?

No.

I hated those dresses. Dad thought girls should be seen and not heard; rosy and unreal. I remember the day I carried a worm to him in my petticoats. I was proud of my find – long and leathery. I held it in the fabric as a sling and staggered over. He threw it at the fence - said I was an embarrassment.

I can still picture the crimson blood of the worm, smearing the wood as it slid down.

He would want me to keep them.

I take the dresses and bin them.

Well, well, well.

Three cases down, I am pleased with my handiwork and considering my next steps. My face cracks into a smile, and I begin to think that yes, I can do this. And none of them are here to stop me, after all.

I can do whatever I want.

Perhaps I would rent a skip. Perhaps I would start a pyre, watch the smoke and secrets disperse on the wind. Flecks. Fumes. Motes. Perhaps I would bury everything, deep, dark, with bare fingers squishing down into the damp earth, not asking, or listening to anyone else. Not caring what they think or want. Not an embarrassment anymore.

And definitely not sorry.

Seven

Adam's Interview

As they waited for the lift, he took in his surroundings. Modern. Clean lines. Bright. And people nodded politely as they passed, he noticed. Nice.

A deferential place.

And good taste too, employing skirt like this secretary. She was fortyish, dressed in trousers… but still… there's no disguising cracking tits and a taut ass.

He could get used to this.

The lift doors opened, and they stepped inside. He watched as she pressed the button for the top floor – nails manicured and pale pink, but short and straight. Shame. He stood behind her, took in the view. A welcome distraction.

"What's your name again?" he asked. She had greeted him at reception and he had been taken aback, expecting the boss, which meant that his well-prepped joke about the local rugby club went to waste. Perhaps he could drop it in later. But of course, he wouldn't meet him. Foolish really. No one with any sense makes their own way down six floors for each candidate.

There was a pause before she answered. A frown. She had a bit of spunk to her, this one. "Jess Hart," she said.

"Miss *Hart*. That rather suits you... So, what's the boss man like? Any tips for me?"

She looked over; momentarily confused.

"You can tell me," he teased.

She didn't respond – eyebrows raised. He winked.

"I should say not," she muttered, eventually.

He chuckled. "Scorpio, right?"

"Pardon?"

"Your star sign… feisty. Strong. A bit of a sting in the tail."

She shuffled. "I can't say I'm into astrology."

He leant in. "But still… Well? I'm right, aren't I?" She looked away, apparently irritated. "I knew it!"

The lift arrived at the top floor, bouncing gently to a standstill.

"Good at reading signs, are you?" she asked. The doors opened. "Straight ahead."

She stood still and gestured for him to leave the lift in front of her.

"Age before beautiful scorpions," he said.

He was still laughing to himself, shaking his head, as he stepped out. Always a good relaxation tool to have a little banter. It had loosened him up.

And then he caught a glimpse of the sign on the office door ahead of them – oak, solid – *Dr Jessica Hart, CEO.*

Eight
Eve's Interview

Not a complete disaster. She hadn't totally humiliated herself. Still, they had all but outright told her she didn't have the job.

Her mobile pinged. Ellie: *Hope it went well don't worry I'm fine xxx*

Perhaps it had been a mistake to mention her own child. She hadn't planned to. But before she knew it, the words had fallen out, one after the other, a string of beads, connected, cascading.

She looked around her, on the bus. It was rare that she was travelling in rush hour. She had imagined it would be full of men in suits, broadsheet newspapers. But no. It wasn't the 1980s, after all. There were teenagers on mobile phones; there was a young man in a trendy suit, trousers narrow, short; a woman with immaculate makeup in some sort of tunic with name badge, reading from an ebook; a mother with a pushchair and a cankerous toddler.

Perhaps she would learn to drive. They hadn't asked that, thank God. It was always humiliating to admit that she couldn't do so by her age. People just assumed that you did, she found. Worse, when they found that she didn't, they seemed to infer that she had lost her licence, somehow.

But no, the truth was more mundane. She was only nineteen when she had Ellie, and hadn't gotten around to it by then. She thought she had all the time in the world. Then, in the following years, the time was never right – she'd have had to pay a babysitter to go for her lessons, so double the cost. And Michael had said it wasn't necessary. She never went far enough on her own for it to be a priority.

Yet how could she travel afar without the means? It all seemed rather chicken and egg, somehow. Not that she would have said so, at the time. It wasn't worth it.

She had been pleased even to get an interview. It was good practice, she told Ellie. She had never had a proper interview. Thirty-four, and she'd never made a formal application for a job, even. Though, of course, she had hoped she wouldn't need the practice. That this would be it.

An elderly lady shuffled towards her and sat in the vacant seat beside her. She smiled and nodded. For a brief moment, speculated that she might have fooled this lady – perhaps fooled them all – into thinking she was a proper grown-up, travelling home from work. A citizen, contributing to society. Making a difference. Or just bloody doing something outside the house, for once.

Just as the internet had predicted, the interview had opened with them asking her about her career to date. She could see they had circled and highlighted things on her C.V. She had talked it all up, as much as she could. But still struggled to think of things to say. There are only so many words you can use to explain that you've been a stay-at-home mum and done some book-keeping and invoicing for your husband for the last fifteen years.

"I see you volunteer for a charity. Why don't you tell us a little about that?" they had prompted.

She felt like a fraud, discussing it, and briefly wondered why she had even put that on the C.V. But the recruitment agency had said it was a good idea to have some different experience. And she did enjoy it, even though Michael had been spitting feathers when she first started.

"Well, I do a lot of it from home. The flexibility suits me. I help with their social media accounts and I monitor the mailbox, reply to general email queries, forwarding things on." She was boring herself.

"And what attracted you to this charity in particular?"

This stumped her. What had attracted her? She paused for a moment – thinking she was silent for a beat too long – and that's when she had started talking about Ellie. How proud she was of her grammar school daughter. How she wanted her to have opportunities she hadn't had. How education has the power to transform people, their lives, so this charity, this organisation supporting girls in developing countries, had struck a chord with her.

"I see." The Deputy Head had nodded. "And is that why you want to work for us, as a Teaching Assistant? This passion for education?"

She should have said 'yes'. She should have told them that she wanted to build on this experience and give something back. She wanted to do something hands-on. She wanted to make a difference, and she felt that she had the skills to do it.

Instead, she told them she needed part-time hours so she could be home in time for her daughter in the evening.

The bus jolted as it pulled up to a stop and a little gaggle of young students got off. Four girls, perhaps twelve, thirteen years old. Laughing as they dismounted, sparkly backpacks adorned with keyrings and badges. They were still out, she considered, after five o'clock. Her reasoning for wanting that job was honest – too honest. But perhaps it was ill-founded.

After that, they had asked her some more targeted questions about the role. She was able to answer the ones about job specifics easily – she had spent the last week pouring over articles, researching, and annotating the Job Description. But she floundered when they gave her a scenario about a disruptive child; and drew a blank when they wanted an example of how she had dealt with a difficult conversation. Michael dealt with the customers. She wasn't to be trusted, apparently. And she wasn't sure a difficult conversation with her soon-to-be-ex-husband was the type of example they were after. Though she had a wealth of those.

At the end, as they were about to leave, the Deputy Head had stopped and paused. She asked her why she had applied for this role specifically, why she hadn't gone for the Administrative Assistant role instead. Her experience aligned more closely with that one, it seemed.

"Well, like I said. I want fewer hours than that. I want to get home –"

"For your daughter. Ah, yes. Shame."

In truth, she did not 'want' fewer hours. She needed all the work she could get. Michael had only just moved out, two, nearly three weeks ago, but already she was feeling the pinch. And it was very likely to get harder before it got better, knowing him.

Her stop was next, so she pressed the bell and pulled herself upright, smiling as she squeezed by the lady next to her, and clutching her new leather attaché bag close to her chest. An impulse purchase – rash really, as she was unlikely to need it soon.

The stop was close to the house. Convenient. It made it easy for her to travel to work without missing too much time at home, she had told Michael. That was over a year ago now, when she had first been brave enough to broach the idea with him. After he had dismissed the idea of the Open University as a waste of time. He told her she was changing.

Not really changing, though. Just being herself.

As she came in the front door a strong acrid smell of garlic hit her. She could hear the radio in the kitchen, Ellie singing along.

"I'm home!" she called.

"Mum!" She came out of the kitchen into the lounge, tea towel in hand. I've started dinner. Come and see."

She wondered what sight would greet her, but the place was remarkably orderly. Pasta ready to boil. Bolognese bubbling. Even a salad in a mixing bowl. Ellie grinned.

"I was about to lay the table."

They leant in to hug each other. "And what have you done with my darling daughter? I should come home late more often."

"I like cooking for you, mum."

She put her bag on a stool and started to unbutton her coat; touched by the scene before her. Tired from the stress of the day. Ellie boiled the kettle then placed the pasta on, to cook.

"How did it go? Was it horrible? I can't believe you did it. I would be wetting myself with nerves."

"I made it to the bathroom, don't worry… It was fine, but it looks like I didn't get it. They told me that they'd be in touch soon as I was the last candidate, and 'if we aren't able to offer you a job on this occasion, please continue to consider us in future'." She made air quotes.

"Oh," Ellie said, frowning. "That's a strange thing to say. What does that mean?"

"Thanks, but no thanks, I think."

Ellie smiled again and gave a small excited jump. "I am so proud of you mum, whatever happens. I know that might sound… you know. Weird or something. But I am."

"Thank you, darling. That means a lot."

She put her things away and splashed her face with cool water. Then she went into the dining room and put the placemats and cutlery on the table. Ellie brought the salad in and told her to stop. To sit down, and let her wait on her.

Her mobile phone rang. The school.

She had been a good candidate, and they liked her. They really did. But there were others with more direct experience who had just pipped her to the post. As she expected.

"There is some good news though, if you will consider it. We have struggled to find appropriate candidates for the Admin Assistant role that I mentioned and we do feel that you would be a very good fit: skills-wise, and with the team. We would like you to consider this role – I'll send the Job Description through... Now, I know what you said about hours, about you needing to be home for your daughter, but perhaps I could ask you to sleep on it?"

Just then, Ellie walked into the room, carrying two bowls of pasta. The sauce smelt deep and rich, and her daughter, her beautiful daughter, tall, independent, grown up, was smiling broadly.

"You know what? Please do send it over. Perhaps I've been too hasty," she said.

Nine

Professor Robertson
Sleeps Away from Home

He turned the chair towards the double doors. The light was off, as were his shoes. Coat on his knees; feet propped on an upended bin. This was as comfortable as he would get.

It was surprisingly peaceful in his office. The floor-length curtains had bobbled, thin fabric, and the moonlight shone through, casting irregular shadows. He left a gap to see outside. A single crisp packet danced and shuffled in the breeze. The quadrangle took on a romance and grace that was missing by day.

He felt an urge to burst out, take in the night air. But there were security cameras. He himself had, once, to review a surprisingly clear tape of footage: a student scribing a tirade against the Vice-Chancellor. He recognised the perpetrator but hadn't said so. The VC was an arse.

But who was he to talk?

A fleeting image of Julianna surfaced. Her face when he left. The unanswered calls.

He wondered if the rat would be back. It came along every night. Obese, leisurely, it was a shockingly confident thing. The first time, he thought it grotesque. But then he had started to become fond of it. Familiarity will do that. His eyes searched for it beneath the silver birch tree.

He could relate to that rat. An outsider, not intentionally harmful. And tubby.

Julianna said she didn't care about his weight. But the fact he was changing: his image, his car – this was a red flag. And when he came home drunk, smelling of new aftershave. Evasive. Well, that told her everything she needed to know.

So she thought.

This would never have come about if it wasn't for Pete. With his arrival came laughter, chaos, and too much wine. He had given him the aftershave. Made him think about his clothes. And taken him to that club.

He'd never been to a gay bar before. He wasn't against homosexuality, but he'd always avoided the topic. Gave it a respectful, but wide berth. But Pete talked openly, matter of fact about his sexuality. Frankly, it was refreshing.

Obviously, he didn't fancy Pete. He didn't fancy blokes. Hadn't. But they'd been to that club, and it was heady, hot. Electrifying. Now he didn't know what to think. Because actually, he felt reborn. Like he was starting to see something new: legs of a fawn, blinking awake. Tentative. Scared. Excited. And he couldn't tell Julianna that, could he?

It was late. He needed to rest, and maybe he'd feel differently when the sun rose. The romance of the quad would be punctured by the sharp yells of teenagers, and his curtains would simply look old, worn, tired.

Yet much later, in the morning, when he woke, he found both the moon and the sun were there. The sunrise was partially obscured by the silver birch, with the unyielding moon holding fast and proud beside it, in the dawn sky. Together.

And scuttling amongst the leaves, visible, exposed, was his tubby little rat.

Ten
Dinner Party

The tagine still smelt peculiar. Even the extra cinnamon had done little to rectify it; Stephanie had hoped it would mask the bitterness. Instead, the whole thing now gave off a stench of hot-cross buns. With tomato chutney.

Bloody Edwin. She knew better than to expect him to shop properly. Even with an itemised list he always came back with one or two items awry. This time it was no honey ("Whoops! Oh well.") and some sort of peculiar smoked garlic paste, instead of a fresh bulb. Apparently, the 'lady in the shop' recommended it. The casserole was already missing the chopped almond its recipe called for, due to Edwin's nut allergy. Three ingredients down, she had added Agave and crossed her fingers.

It hadn't worked.

This didn't bode well for the evening, which she was already dreading. It was his idea. They were his colleagues. So how was it that she was stuck in the kitchen, hoping the rather expensive lamb she had used would somehow compensate for other second-rate – or absent - ingredients?

She felt like a child, pretending to be a grown-up. And she knew her problems were ludicrous. First world. Petty. Middle-class. But it still rankled.

Edwin wandered into the kitchen, shirtless, for no apparent reason. He smelt of 80s aftershave with a backdrop of body odour. He hadn't bothered to shower. She winced.

He was humming to himself, as he opened the cupboard to fetch a wine glass – one that didn't match the set she had already placed on the table – and then grabbed the Chablis from the fridge.

"Can't you lubricate yourself with the Pinot?" she asked. He ignored her and cracked the cap open. "It's already open." She gestured towards the fridge with a knife. He stopped, and stared at the blade, pointedly. She turned back to the meal.

"Do you want some?" he asked, lightly, after a beat.

"I bought that one especially." She turned again, and made a move to swipe the Chablis from him, half-heartedly. "For the guests."

"I don't believe in keeping things for best."

"That's right. You just do whatever the hell you want, don't you?" she muttered, turning back.

He laughed: deep. Booming. Fake. "Love you too, my darling."

Stephanie glanced at her phone. Seven o'clock. She had thirty minutes, if that, to get ready.

***

Twenty minutes later, the doorbell rang. A mist of sweat had settled across her hairline while she had rushed to

32

get ready, cracking and smudging her makeup and curling the little wisps at the nape of her neck. Old. She was getting old.

She had no jewellery on, no tights, no shoes. She called to Edwin to get the door. No response. This would have to do.

It was Annabel, his Assistant. She was a little thing, twenty-five, if that. Stephanie took in the three-inch heels, the sparkling, deep-green dress that flashed beneath her black coat, the matching eye shadow. She had made an effort.

She was holding a bottle of prosecco, clutching it tightly with both hands. Annabel gave a nervous grin, in a twitchy sort of way, then looked over her left shoulder down the street.

"Ben is just parking the car," she said.

Stephanie realised she hadn't spoken; hadn't even smiled. No wonder the poor girl looked nervous.

"Yes, yes, come in, come in!" She overcompensated, gesturing into the hallway, and beaming.

"Well, I'd better wait for him, hadn't I?"

"We will leave the door ajar. He'll find us."

Stephanie reached forward to usher her in and take the wine, which Annabel misread as a hug, leaving them to hopscotch a few awkward steps and air kisses in the doorway.

Edwin and Ben appeared almost simultaneously from behind each of the women as they ended their dance.

"There she is!" Edwin bellowed.

He was wearing a deep pink silk shirt, which clung to his skin in unfortunate places and emphasised the blood vessels in his eyes. Ben wore a soft green jumper, with a high neck, matching Annabel's outfit, she realised. The patterned collar of his shirt poked out, tastefully. Cotton.

Stephanie took Annabel's coat, wine, and the bunch of lilies that Ben produced. Edwin led the way to the alcohol while she hung the coat under the stairs, then took the gifts into the kitchen.

"I'd best get on with the starters," she called to them as she walked through the lounge. Edwin continued with his story about the sherry he was offering them, leaving Annabel and Ben to nod and smile back and forth between him and Stephanie.

Sherry. For twenty-five-year-olds.

Fifteen minutes later, and she was unfettering an avocado from its skin when an athletic-looking woman with short, black hair strode into the kitchen.

"Something smells good," she said. "Can I help?"

She placed a bottle of red wine on the side and started to unbutton her jacket, purposefully.

"Oh no, all under control."

"That's a relief." She smiled. "I'm a shocking cook." She leant against the oven and then jumped back in surprise from the heat, then laughed at herself, pointing at the appliance, and shaking her head.

"You must be Rose," Stephanie said. "I would shake hands but I'm in avocado hell at the moment."

Rose nodded. "Have you got a drink to ease the pain?"

"No, looks like I've missed out on that front."

"Tut, tut. I shall reprimand him."

"You could get the Chablis from the fridge if you like? I'm more than happy to skip the aperitif." She wrinkled her nose. "…Oh, that is, if you are?"

"Sure," Rose said. "In here?" She made her way to the fridge, placing her jacket down on a bar stool as she did so. She was shorter than Stephanie, and perhaps five, eight years younger, with tanned, makeup-free skin. She wore a loose, knee-length smock dress and flat, chunky loafers. The edge of a small, black tattoo poked out from under one sleeve. Stephanie breathed a sigh of relief – first impressions of Edwin's new boss were favourable. Perhaps the night would be better than she had feared.

***

They were already three bottles down by the time the tagine came out from the kitchen. Ben had been persuaded to leave his car, which seemed a sensible idea seeing as Edwin had spent much of the previous hour quizzing him about everything from his job to his taste in suits.

"Leave the poor boy alone," cried Stephanie, placing a large bowl of couscous in front of Edwin. "And serve your guests."

"Just making sure that he is good enough for our precious Ani," he replied, picking up the ladle.

A grimace fluttered across his face, and she wondered, again, if he had feelings for Annabel - something she had banished from her thoughts months ago. This was during the period when she was still in shock. Burnt. Wounded. When she had been trying to make sense of his behaviour, unpick his stories to reveal the truth. But the truth didn't involve Annabel. She knew that now.

No doubt his grimace was at the couscous.

She turned back to the tagine, removed the lid of the pot. Ben, sat beside her where she stood, tugged her sleeve gently.

"It looks lovely, but I'll have to give it a pass, I'm afraid. I'm a vegetarian." He was apologetic, speaking in hushed tones.

Stephanie dropped the spoon into the casserole dish with a clatter and stared at Edwin, who looked up.

"Steady on, girl," he said.

"I'm so sorry, Ben. I had no idea." Her words were hard little stones that plopped from her mouth. She had asked him. Repeatedly. He had said he would check.

"What's this?" Edwin said, wet mouthed, too loud.

Ben lifted his hands, mea culpa. "It's my fault for being the awkward one. Couscous is fine. Don't worry about me."

"Oh! Never mind. More meat for the rest of us," said Edwin, dishing the semolina onto Ben's plate. "Here, you can have my couscous."

***

Stephanie decided to tune Edwin out and make the most of the company. She managed to settle into conversation with Rose, even though she was sat across from her, and Edwin's strident anecdotes, told to poor Annabel and Ben, overlaid everything they said.

She had been at Johnson and Howe for six months, but various members of the team had been taking it in turns to work from home for at least the first two of those. She was new to the town, new to the company, and was refreshingly candid about how anxious this made her feel. Grateful for Edwin's invitation. It was the first time she'd socialised since a flying visit from her sister two months ago.

Rose looked over to Edwin and smiled softly, and it struck Stephanie that she thought of Edwin as her friend, and that he had held this party to be kind.

Kind? Stephanie assumed an ulterior motive. She couldn't imagine him enjoying the company of this confident, modern woman. His first-ever female line manager. He had been quite scathing when she had been appointed, she recalled.

Rose told her about her old role and the differences between that company and this. She talked about a 'toxic environment' and the challenges she had faced, while Stephanie picked at her food and topped up their glasses. Stephanie herself had worked at Johnson and Howe until eighteen months earlier. She thought, perhaps, that Rose was still in a honeymoon phase. But she said nothing.

She listened, vaguely detached, while Rose spoke with her decisive, steady tones, and Edwin blared at the others, hardly drawing a breath.

It would have been a pleasant evening without him, she considered. How odd to think that. But it was true.

She picked up her plate and excused herself, started to stack the others' dishes to clear the table. She noted how Annabel's black eyeliner had smudged in the corners, and how Ben had loosely placed his arm around the back of her chair, leaning in towards her, comfortably.

They had been like that, once. For years, in fact. They were the couple who didn't care about public displays of affection. Who held hands as they walked in the streets. Who teased one another, laughed at each other's jokes.

They were in love. Deeply in love. For over two decades. How had it come to this?

She picked up Edwin's plate and looked at him, was about to smile, when he glanced away, eyes glazed, and started a new anecdote.

***

Annabel was talking about wanting children, and how multiple births ran in her family. Ben was laughing, pretending to hold his head in his hands in horror, as she described how her second cousin had not one, but two sets of twins. This morphed into a conversation about children's names and whether it was cruel or a matter of personal freedom to give children unusual names.

"Thank God we never had to worry about that," Edwin said, raising his glass in a sort of toast.

Stephanie flinched.

Rose caught her eye and asked if she wanted a top-up. She smiled weakly at the woman, nodding her thanks, ashamed as her eyes brimmed.

"I'd best put the pudding in," she said, excusing herself from the table.

She was placing the second bread pudding in the oven when Rose walked in with both their wine glasses.

"You're going to get me drunk," Stephanie said.

"I'm hoping you'll spill all his innermost secrets. Give me the upper hand." She smiled, gave an exaggerated wink. Stephanie took her glass.

"He doesn't have any inner secrets," Stephanie answered, flatly. "What you see is what you get."

They both stood still, in silence for a moment.

"It's not that we can't have kids. He didn't want them."

"Hey, you don't need to explain anything to me," Rose said, lifting one hand. She took a step backwards.

Was she oversharing? Probably. She didn't care.

"I did. When we met, at least… in the beginning, I secretly wanted them, and I thought he might change his mind. Stupid, really. He didn't. Obviously," she laughed, sardonically. "Anyway, I made a choice. I loved him more than I loved the idea of children."

Rose nodded. Stephanie wondered if she had noticed the past tense.

***

Ben, Rose, and Edwin were all in the garden, smoking. Annabel was talking and slurring, leaning across the table, head resting on one hand. She had plaited her hair and kept trying to tie a knot in it, to keep off her face, but she was failing, and it repeatedly fell down and forward across her forehead as she spoke. Stephanie noticed that she had a new pimple appearing on her chin and that she had lost a false nail, revealing brutally chewed nails beneath, raw and pink.

She was so incredibly young. How had she ever thought Edwin was interested in her? Or more accurately, she in him? But no, she had been right to. It would be classic Edwin to do something like that. To fall for the pretty secretary. Classic bloody Edwin. And he had been behaving strangely, or differently, at least – and working longer hours. She wasn't totally foolish to wonder if he was having an affair. They were classic signs.

But it was his new boss, ringing the changes, setting higher expectations. That was all. Good for her. And he probably revelled in the opportunity to stay away from home; she could hardly blame him for that.

Ben wandered back in. "Is there something in the oven?" he asked.

"Damn it!" she cried.

***

The bread pudding was finished, and Edwin had insisted on making the coffee. He made a show of it, repeating how she must sit and let him do it. As if she had been declining offers of help all day. But he had made none.

Ben was asking Rose how she found the move – where she had come from, and where she grew up. She had moved around a little, she said. She'd been single for years and loved to live alone. She had freedom.

"I don't trust easily. Product of a broken home," she said.

"Aren't we all?" muttered Ben.

"Ah, but I bet your dad didn't have affairs with multiple members of your extended family," Rose countered.

"Hopefully, his wife's cousins, rather than his own?" Ben asked.

"Yup. But not just cousins."

Stephanie was taken back to that night three months ago when Edwin had not come home until 3.30 am. Phone switched off. No explanation. That was when it had solidified, this feeling. When she had fallen down, into the hole. That was the moment when she could no longer pretend.

"Tell me about Johnson and Howe," Stephanie interrupted. "I'm out of touch. Any gossip?"

"Gossip? Not that I know of. But I could be the wrong person to ask." Rose shuffled in her seat. Perhaps she had overstepped. But she persisted, anyway. Now or never.

"Any new staff? There must be some bright young things there now. I know there have been some retirements."

"Arthur is nice," said Annabel. "And what's-her-name. You know…" she circled one finger in the air, struggling to recall the name. "The gorgeous one."

"Oh, I know. She's called Annabel," said Ben, leaning into her.

"Bethany," said Rose, looking down at the table.

Just then, Edwin came in with a cafetiere of coffee and a carton of milk. No jug. He looked at Rose.

"No more work talk, please," he said. "Who else would like one more cheeky smoke while the coffee brews?"

"I will," said Rose.

***

They were on the brandy and amaretto now, but Stephanie had drunk more than enough, so she had taken herself off to the kitchen. She started to rinse the easiest dishes in the sink to clear some space. The place was a disaster – the thought of greeting the mess with a hangover was enough to spur her on to make a dent in it. Besides, Annabel was talking babies again.

The thought came to her again. That same, bitter little thought that she couldn't seem to stop from resurfacing, once a week. No, almost once a day. Two decades she had been with this man – she had given him her youth. She had given up her hopes. If she left him now – what was it for? If they broke up, it was too late for her. That time was gone. But not too late for him.

She felt trapped.

Perhaps this was a middle-life crisis. Perhaps this was what that felt like. Perhaps it was her, not him. Hormones. Ageing. Fear. Maybe he was doing nothing – had done nothing, after all.

Rose came into the kitchen again. "Ed is asking if there is more bread pudding."

"Ed?" She had never called him that.

"Shall I just take the dish?" Rose stretched her strong, lean arm out to grab it.

"No," Stephanie turned, soapy glass in hand, "Not that one. That's the pecan one. I made two."

A small, puzzled pinch appeared between Rose's eyebrows. "He doesn't like pecans? The fool!"

"Ha! No. He's terribly allergic. I don't even eat nuts when I'm around him. That's pecan and maple. But we've got a different one, see?" Stephanie gestured to the smaller pan to the right.

"Oh, I didn't know…"

"Don't even share a bed or get too close when I have eaten nuts. Can't even risk a kiss. Not that there's too much of that going on these days." She turned back towards the sink.

Then Annabel wobbled into the kitchen. Her reedy, slushy voice was anxious and high. "There's something wrong with Edwin," she said. "He needs an… an epi-pen?"

Stephanie turned back, a wave of confusion hitting her. Then she caught sight of Rose. She was standing stock still, mouth dropped slightly ajar, eyes wide, unblinking. Looking at Stephanie. Staring. Aghast.

Then the wine glass slipped from her grip and hit the kitchen floor, and shattered into a dozen pieces.

Ten
Cashier Number Four

Susan sat down at check-out number four, rearranging the seat height with one hand, and grabbing a bottle of sanitiser with the other. She had her routine down. It was a little like starting a car: checking mirrors, changing heater settings, emptying the cash into the till. That sort of thing. She'd been doing this for seven years. The longest-standing check-out staff in the shop.

Not exactly the most prestigious accolade.

Before she'd even started to wipe down the conveyor, shoppers started to close in. Like herring gulls, they were. Beady eyes spotting her straight away. Taking a chance. Hopping closer. Impatient.

She turned on the light above her till and moved the 'Check-out Closed' sign out of the way.

The first customer only had a handful of produce, which he clutched against his chest, both before and after purchase. Not wanting the inconvenience of a basket, or the cost of a bag, presumably. If he could, he'd have had her scanning them in his arms.

He didn't make eye contact; didn't answer her "Have a nice day." It was all over in a few moments.

That wasn't a good start. If he'd been buying more, she'd have been tempted to 'accidentally' scan through one of his expensive goods a couple of times too many. But as it was, he'd have noticed. That only works on the big shops.

The next customer was still laying her goods out, so Susan paused, smiled, held the margarine ready to scan but gave the poor lady a breather. She smiled back at her and nodded her thanks. Susan liked that. Made a mental note to accidentally-on-purpose fail to scan one of the more costly items in her haul.

Next came a young mum. She had a newborn strapped to her chest and a toddler in the trolley seat. At first glance, she looked like she was coping admirably, as the kids had coordinated outfits and expensive shoes. But Susan knew where to look for the signs: nails painted but badly chipped. Coat on the kids, but not on herself. That sort of thing. Her eye makeup was clumpy and smudged: yesterday's, no doubt.

There was a lot of shopping to get through so Susan switched off and swiped away, while her mind drifted. She couldn't stop thinking of the words she'd had with him downstairs this morning. Brian. She could hear the voices as soon as she stepped out of her flat: two, maybe three men. Though by the time she was at the front door, Brian was standing alone on the threshold: spread-eagle like a spiderweb blocking the way. All legs and elbows.

"Fucking Prosecco Poofs!" he was yelling, to the back of a young man who was striding away.

"Excuse me," Susan said.

Brian turned around, wild-eyed.

"Did you hear them, last night?" he asked.

"I'm sorry, who?"

"The la-di-dah lads in number one," he spat.

"What do you mean?" Susan asked, genuinely confused.

"Them." He waved vaguely outside. "The boys. Their party. Crap dance music and a flat full of them."

"Ah, no," Susan said, stepping past him. "I'm on the top floor. I didn't hear a thing… but didn't you get their note?"

"Oh yeah." He chuckled, humourlessly. "I got their 'note'."

She turned towards him. "Well then, at least we were warned. It was a wedding party. Can't begrudge them a bit of noise on that occasion."

"A gay wedding isn't a wedding in my book. And giving me a note doesn't mean you've got my blessing."

She turned away; cheeks warm. "Oh well. Live and let live, I say."

"Fucking Prosecco Poofs," he answered.

The young woman's shopping was all scanned and Susan smiled at her as she loaded the last of her bags back into the trolley. No wedding ring, she noticed.

She couldn't say she really understood it, the way these young people thought. The way they lived. And in truth, it did make her feel a little awkward when she met those young men together in a pair. But they seemed nice enough, and they clearly doted on one another. No harm done. None of her business. Why people had to get so het up about other people's choices she could never understand.

She was pulled up out of her thoughts by the next customer. He was loading the last of his shopping onto the belt while chewing the ear off someone on his mobile phone. She asked him if he needed any bags, and he waved her away like a fly.

"I tell you. I'm not doing it again. They bloody rearrange this place every two minutes. Stand still long enough and they'll move the biscuits right in front of your eyes… No. Like hell it has. It was only two weeks ago I helped you with the shopping. Last month! You must be--"

He came around to the other end, to start packing his shopping. Susan continued to bleep things through, nonchalantly.

"Oh yeah, that's right you 'don't feel well'. I'll give something to-" He looked up at Susan briefly and caught her eye. She looked away. "Anyway, I got eggs. You can do egg and chips tonight… what?... Oh, don't be so bloody… You've never said that before. I think I'd remember if you'd told me you didn't like bloody eggs. You're just… Right. Anyway. I've got to go and pack this bloody shopping I've done for you."

He took the phone from his ear and disconnected.

Susan continued to swipe the shopping through, leaving the eggs until last. Finally, she picked the carton up and gave a cursory glance at the eggs inside. As she closed them, she stared vacantly, straight ahead. Then she took her index finger and slid it under the lid, pressing down until she felt a satisfying 'chink' beneath her skin as the eggshell crumbled. She closed the lid and passed them to him.

"That'll be £59.87," she said.

Next came an elderly lady with a basket full of vegetables. She was clutching a purse and frowning. She came in every Sunday, that one. Counted her coins to pay. One time, she even had to put something back. Susan didn't bother her with any chitchat but was careful to make sure that she didn't quite let any of the bags of fruit or veg rest properly on the scales. Just a few ounces off each one. Only a little.

She watched the woman walking out of the shop, keeping an eye because the floor outside was wet. She heard the sound of someone clearing their throat, nearby. Looked up.

It was flipping Brian.

He nodded.

Susan started to scan his shopping and he moved to the end to pack his bags. He was one of those who thinks he is a superior shopper, had it all worked out. You know the type, makes a big deal out of having a system. Even remembers to bring insulated bags for his frozen goods.

Mind you, there were an awful lot of cheap pizzas and ready meals amongst his things. And alcohol.

"Live and let live," she whispered to herself, in an effort to keep her judgement at bay.

Perhaps she said it a little louder than she had intended as she could have sworn she heard him mutter: "Live and let bloody die."

As she made her way towards the end of the shopping, she noted a bottle of Prosecco amongst the multipacks of own-brand crisps. She paused briefly and snorted, involuntarily. She looked up. He stared at her, eyes narrow, daring her to say something, but she took the crisps and scanned them, sliding them down towards him just a little too briskly so that they slid off the side and fell to the floor.

"Oh dear," she said, flatly.

He bent down to retrieve them, muttering to himself.

Then she smiled gently to herself and took the bottle of Prosecco in her hands.

Thank you for reading my book. If you have enjoyed it, please leave me a review. You have no idea the difference this can make.

Thank you also to my early readers, and every one of my supportive friends.

.

Little Gems and Riches

The opening story from The Blue Hour, *my first collection. Part two of this story appears in* The Day I Nearly Drowned.

Arthur walked past me, carrying a cup of tea, flickering, tremoring – the mug ready to turn as a shooting star. He made it to the sideboard and placed it down (too heavily) on a coaster beside me.

'Humph,' he said. He did not look at me.

He turned back to make the long journey to the kitchen again. He shuffled in his pyjama bottoms, feet poking out from open slippers, nails and toes both peeling like baby snail shells. This was the indignity of having to move.

By the time he had found his way back to me, he had left a trail of tea splatters on the carpet and he was red – crimson - in the face.

'There we are, then,' he said, with his gruff affection. He waved his hand as if to pat me on the leg. 'There we are.'

He took a sip of his tea. I could see it was too strong, and it looked to me as if it was made in the cup, not the pot. It put me off glancing at my own. I didn't want him to think me ungrateful. I knew what it had taken him to make it.

'It's nice to see you,' he stated, 'Nice when you come around. You know.'

He took a deep swig. It must have been too hot. Would have burnt his mouth, I was sure.

We sat for a little while in silence. I could feel the weight of his body on the couch, almost pressed against me, shifting the cushions, and warming me up. He was quite close; I liked it. I could even smell the tea on his breath.

After a little while, he shuffled himself upright. He rocked his body back and forth, long arms pressed down hard into the sofa cushions - an octogenarian chimpanzee - until he finally swung into an upright position. Once upright he stood for a moment. He swayed. Then he grabbed the remote control from the occasional table and jabbed at it, to turn on the television; I knew this was for my benefit though once it sprung to life it was so quiet, I could barely hear it.

Then he was off again: an unsteady potter.

'Must get the dinner on,' I heard him mutter.

It was only half past four.

I watched him come in and out of the kitchen, back and forth half a dozen times, until on the dining table he placed two knives, two forks. A pair of coasters. Salt and pepper. Two glasses. A miniature world in binary.

***

After something different? Dreena also writes contemporary genre fiction under Jane Harvey, with her first novel, The Landlord of Hummingbird House.

Printed in Great Britain
by Amazon

13976686R00041